Handy Mr Hippo

Written by Chae In-seon

Illustrated by Kim You-dae

Edited by Joy Cowley

Mr Hippo is a handy hippo.
He fixes everything.

"I have no hot water! Can you come?"
Mr Hippo says, "I will be right there."

"My refrigerator is not working."
"Okay, I'll fix it," Mr Hippo says.

Mr Hippo is a happy hippo.

Everyone likes him.

He says, "How are you?

What can I do for you today?"

When he is done, he says,
"Bye! Just give me a call
when you need me again."

One night, Mr Hippo got a call.

"This is the hairy giant," said a voice.

Mr Hippo was startled.

The hairy giant was a mean giant.

"Come tomorrow morning!"
said the hairy giant.
"Nearly everything in my house
is broken and needs to be fixed."
"OK, I will come tomorrow morning,"
said a worried Mr Hippo.

When Mr Hippo got to the giant's house,
the hairy giant was mean and angry.
"You little hippopotamus! You are late!
I can't do anything because of you!"

"Let me see," said Mr Hippo.

The house was full of broken things.

Mr Hippo didn't know where to start.

The first thing to be fixed
was the hairy giant's shaver.

The next thing to be fixed
was the refrigerator.
The giant was happy
that he could use it again.

13

Mr Hippo fixed the washing machine,
and the giant did his laundry.
Mr Hippo fixed the oven,
and the giant had a meal.

The next day, Mr Hippo fixed
the fan and the television.

Mr Hippo worked hard.
There was one chair left to fix.
The hairy giant was thankful for
all Mr Hippo had done.

16

"May I go home now?"
said Mr Hippo.
"Of course you may,"
said the giant.

17

As Mr Hippo walked away,
the giant yelled, "Wait!
I have a question to ask.
Why does everyone run away
when they see me?"

Wait!

"Oh that!" said Mr Hippo.

"I can fix that, too.

Just repeat after me…

How are you? Welcome!
Bye! Have a nice day!
Please come again!"

Mr Hippo's friends
were worried about Mr Hippo.
So they came to the giant's house.

22

The hairy giant greeted them
with a big smile. "How are you?
Nice to meet you. Welcome!"

23

The animals were surprised.
"Mr Hippo is very handy,"
they said. "Look! He has even fixed
the mean hairy giant."

The giant laughed and said,
"Thanks for coming to my house.
Please come inside."

"We will have a party."

Dear Mr Hippo,

I was a mean giant.
Everyone ran away from me.
You showed me how to use nice words.
Now I am not mean.
I have a big smile.
Everyone likes to come to my house.
Thank you, Mr Hippo!
Have a nice day! Bye!

From the hairy giant

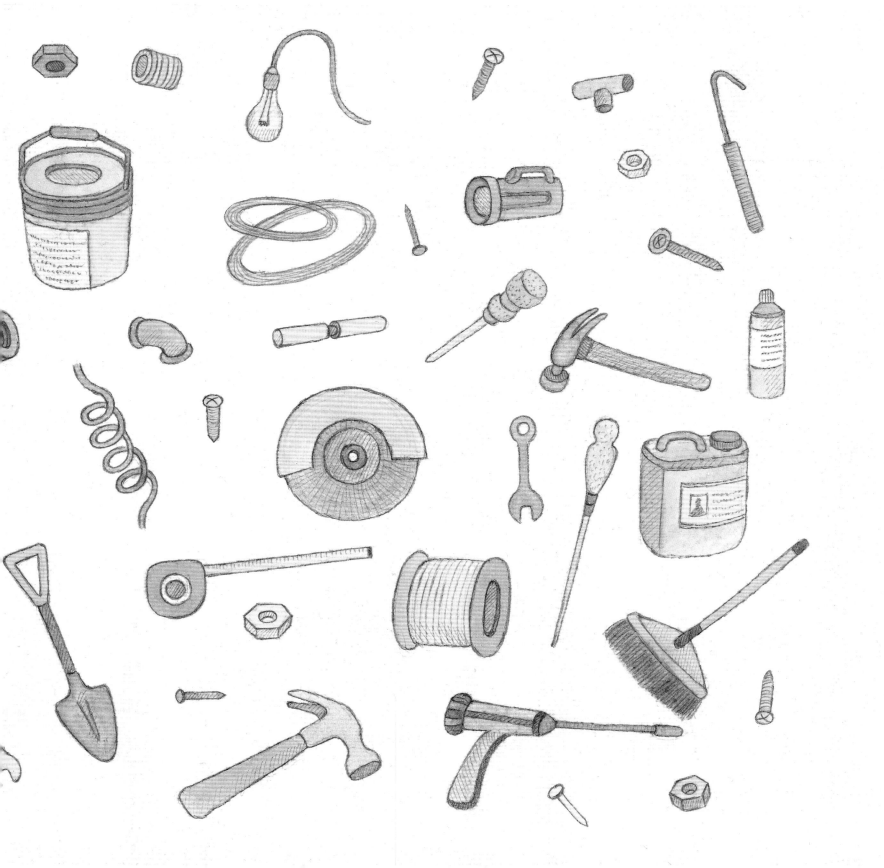

big & SMALL

Original Korean text © Chae In-seon
Illustrations © Kim You-dae
Original Korean edition © Sigongsa 2000

This English edition published by Big & Small in 2015
by arrangement with Sigongsa
English text edited by Joy Cowley
Additional editing by Mary Lindeen
Artwork for this edition produced
in cooperation with Norwood House Press, USA
English edition © Big & Small 2015

ISBN: 978-1-925233-98-8

Printed in Korea